The Rambling Hand

Richard MacNeill

The Rambling Hand

Perhaps, it is simply for each of us to live our role in the world, whatever it may be. "Act well your part; there all the honour lies." Yet realize, while the role is a part, we are whole. Seemingly certainly true, yet there is much more to existing, to first discovering, which rises from one's highest vision, one's purpose. To exist, to be, to really live. For the ones who see, there is a knowing, the inner light, the ultimate best, the calling.

Imagination exceptional, the connection never fading with age, though the roughness of experience may make foggy the unseen true. Maturity with the gift of the fantastic, the original child's gift. Good way for a writer to be. Write what you experience, imagine more, go deeper. We are story. No one knows. Some acceptance can continue as the bare minimum to not set the world on fire. All may be imagination. For a seeker, the delver into existence, all is conjecture and anything is possible. Reality is ready to crumble at any moment, with phantoms dancing sarcastic on the rubble. One may go into realms with the very soul as the barriers melt away, as oneself melts away the barriers. Then what, allow yet another maze to erect? All boundaries are internally present; any physical appearance of such simply shows what is within.

Scenarios of quality are functional necessities. Take a break and start over. Is this craft important at all, or are we scraping ink onto a dead tree's ass? Romantic view, acknowledge the art weaving magic with the written word, storyteller. Optimistically inspired, free. But the low points which gulp so low after soaring so high, when the world seems everything but a fitting place, it is not a fitting place. You are sent to live among them for a time, but you are not of them. Bring your own world into this where you do not fit. Don't force yourself into a puzzle, and don't submit to their jumble of missing pieces. Who would pass as scum at the bottom of a lake?

What a mess the head gets in, back and forth. Exeunt worry from the windows of your mind and breathe in the light of nature's beauty. Writing singes pages, always a ridiculous rambling. A frantic hummingbird tries to get out through a closed window after wandering on the wing into the house. There can be some oddness stranded in the pen which releases things coming not from the mind. Stories coming out of somewhere, or nowhere.

Life is stories forever. Imagining endless lounges and freakshows. From the writer's hand is eternity expressed, the mighty mountains and ravenous ravines, infinite song of conflict and peace. Inkstains on fingers and every moment more of reality, less of reality. All is possible and all is passing. He drinks wine with Khayyam, alone or with good friends, smoking the hookah with a caterpillar.

They are dumbfounded by a home with no television. Growing up, having one to watch as much as anyone, which was always too much, while nature's heart looked upon the seen and unseen, not to be lost in the screen. How can you live? What do you do? Achieve all living when not zoned out in constant distracting noise.

The love of walking, owning a car which is rarely used, occasional bike riding for the fun of the feeling, the point of the day is not to speed through, but to enjoy the experience. To do what intensely must be done, to accept the gifts of the Great Song's wisdom and love all, to gift these necessities of loving to the ones who are learning the way, enthusiastically making truth's continuum, living completely by the craft of one's will.

Pierce through. What anxiety creeps in is of our toilsome sadness. Justice gives way to primitivism, which then rises to ideals of honor and truth. The scope of humankind's intellectual and emotional history is in daily discovery. It is for some to leap in, to swim the great undulating waves of the Mystery, then upon returning to the shore seeing the eternal wisdom is rejected, mistaken and distorted, or clung to firmly as immovable paradigm. All the while the seer on the shore is outcast on the edge of impermanence. They may call his adventure and exploration brave, they may call it foolish. What some see as brave/foolish, this one sees as itself.

They reside semi-comfortably inside the grand walled city of civilization. One may venture out, feel a strong wind blowing eastward, and return to tell the rest what he thinks he has learned. They may take it as divine and inscribe it on the walls. A seer remains outside and they call him mad, for he tells how the wind blows in every direction and their scribbled doctrines mean nothing.

Always wilderness. Those who stay locked away, they are yet wilderness and have the natural potential. Nature is. Hearts are born from, return to, and are always within the Original. Pathless and barefoot the seer wanders, skirting the boundaries, passing through connections where no boundaries exist, treading lightly among ruins and eventual ruins. Breathing the eternal, blood moving infinite, whose eyes see what cannot be looked for nor explained.

We need not revolve in society's rebuke and adoration. Why? Freedom. Might some well be vicious, as well as any tiger might be. To live life in uncompromising freedom, nothing obstructing the pure and intelligent right, wild and true, to think and observe, with patience for sight. This is the obsession with the pirate and the kraken by those who wonder in fear and sarcasm at anything deeper than a basket of french fries, who seek nothing and merely exist, living vicariously through those who are free. Such grand ideas as oceans and stars are held in awe by those who have capacity for awe. We are as grand as oceans and stars in the whole sustaining universe.

Life doesn't feel forced when you're at peace where you're meant to be. Full of goodness and constant inspiration. The sense of unity and belonging in the universe. The unimportant shields its eyes from the light above, where you are.

In transitions, change in great flurries, and the trees

with good roots sway while staying secure. Autumns of life come, often unexpectedly tearing leaves from our branches. Darkening then to winter, prevailing through the season returns to spring.

No era was the one of true place for anyone. Clean away the wrongs in your heart. Replace anger with acceptance, replace endless distaste with open ears. Outcast may be destined, but happiness is attainable. Anywhen and where in the universe is born the chance for happiness.

Tell me a story

Once upon a time, there was a rat named Turtledove. Miserable in the city, in the nasty wet sewers and alleys, he travelled to the forest.

Why are you going to the forest? The ratpack laughed, *You don't know what you're doing.*

The forest is where we're from, he said, *and I'm not happy here.*

Goodbye, they waved sarcastically as he went.

In the forest he travelled alone and smiling, but not realizing how quickly he would become lonely. Night felt a newcomer and an owl silently roared down upon him. Scared and lifted into a tree, the rat was momentarily gleeful he'd die by a hungry bird in the forest and not by an angry stranger's stomping foot, or a wheel crushing him as it sped too close to the gutter, or a drowning coagulation of feasting rats whose tails were tangled while they fed in the muck and couldn't shake free, or sickness, or careless freezing cardboard graves too full and too demanding of more.

The owl clutched him onto a branch and looked close. *You probably taste like crap*, it said.

The rat was upset that the owl could say those offensive words to an animal over which it had power, who would take him from his wandering, who would shuck meals praying to be dead before they ride to its guts. He began to speak out, but the bird wasn't listening and released its grip.

Turtledove ran down the tree and nearly tripped over a hole in his climb, grabbing onto the bark before falling from the canopy to the unseen blackness. From the sudden nest peered a beautiful girl rat, who lifted him up, and he thanked her. They walked along the branches. She showed him the best food and the necessity of safety. From that night on, they remained with each other, talking, laughing, foraging, and living happily ever after.

The Tea-Giver

Civil war, the people's unrest,
the battling had been on for some time.
There was contention and
there was bloodshed and
there was a man from the mountains.
Now, three men dressed in white
and three men dressed in black
were fighting in the hills
when up strolled the man
with a sack over his shoulder.
He sat down in the grass
not far from their fight
and poured hot water over tea.
When a tunic of white
and a tunic of black
came at once to inquire,
they were invited to sit.
Because tea was sacred
to all in this land,
they accepted and
thanked the odd man.
Soon, the others came
and began a heated quarrelling
while the man sipped
and smiled at the clouds.
A white-clad man
yelled his reasons for war,
then turned to the tea-giver and asked,
"Well, what do you think of it all?"
His reply was short,
"How's your tea?"
The soldier was stunned and puzzled,
"Delicious, thank you."
Then a black-clad soldier
gave his reasons of grudge,

and turned to the tea-giver to ask,
"What do you think of all that?"
To which his reply was simple,
"How's your tea?"
Shocked as the other,
the soldier answered,
"It's delicious, thank you."
They sat a few moments in rigid silence,
the odd man still gazing at the sky.
Suddenly, he pointed to a cloud
and shouted, "Look, a bunny rabbit!"
The others looked up.
"Oh, I see it!"
"There are its ears!"
"And its fluffy tail!"
The tea-giver laughed
and soon began
gathering his sack to be on.
Hugging each with friendly farewell,
he said, "The next time you boys
feel like fighting each other,
don't forget to stop and have tea."

Red Mountain

-is not the kind of place you go on vacation. They call the old mining camp a "living ghost town", but the pleasant t-word isn't fitting. It's a scattered population of shanties and isolated creatures who sport an epidermis of sand, all of whom I met were very kind folk.

Hiking alone, I made my way around the far side of the hills where no one goes, the gates of mineshafts left standing like ancient ruined altars to goblintown. Trekking hidden corners of the desert I'd not yet seen, misfortune came at its leisurely, inconvenient pace. The asshole bit me in the leg. I snatched him up, surprised by my own quickness, and held him tight below the head with my thumb pressing into his throat. We looked at each other until he stopped wiggling. Then, I whipped his head into the dirt.

The snake clenched in my grip, I hobbled through the sharp brush and thorns toward where the nearest humans might be. There was a shack with welcoming energy, or perhaps I welcomed any sign of help, even a shack in the middle of the desert. I knocked on the screen door and was quickly answered by a short man limping on a gnarled crutch. He wasn't wearing much, no shoes, torn jean shorts, and a sleeveless pink fish-net. I tried to speak. The poison was running strong. I wasn't able to form words and stumbled to the ground in sudden weakness. Holding the snake and pointing to my leg -

I woke up beneath a gently waving eagle's wing. I lifted my head and tried to sit up, but a hand touched my chest and I heard a raspy voice tell me to lay back down. The air was thick with sage smoke and I was drenched in sweat. A large old lady was mumbling as she waved the heavy feathers.

I must've passed out again. When I awoke, sunlight was blazing through the thin curtains. The desert's heat crushed my body like a giant's grip. I hadn't gathered my mind yet when the old woman came in. "Good boy," she said, "you're awake. Come on out here." Slowly, I walked through the hall to the other room and saw, as she sat in her chair, we were in a single-wide trailer. Standing in the room was a man who looked like the security guard of the boonies. Big knife on his belt, dark hair, pointed black boots, his whole person incredibly dirty and incredibly confident. The old woman handed me a cup of water, warm and stale, but appreciated nonetheless. Then, the man placed a beer in my hand, which was mildly cold, and we sat on the couch.

"Do you know how you got here?" the old woman asked. No, I said, and she motioned to the man, "Jackrabbit brought you to me."

I thanked him and he told me, "She's a medicine woman."

Then, she pointed to my leg, "Wrap it only in the bandage I used." I realized there was no pain and I felt excellent considering the circumstances. I was struck by the immediate desire to be on my way home, but I felt so thankful and didn't want to be rude.

"Medicine Woman, tell him a story." Jackrabbit suggested.

I sat and listened as they spun tales which bound together interconnecting strands. We sat a long time, until the sun grew orange in the windows. I was reaching the point where I would dare to politely interrupt them, for they hadn't stopped talking, and say it was time for me to go. Sensing the end of my patience and courtesy, Jackrabbit stood and offered to take me to my car. I shook hands with the woman and she eased the anxiety lurking under my gratitude. "Jackrabbit has something for you."

The man in the pink fish-net had crutched his fastest to Jackrabbit's hovel, who lifted my unconscious body into the cab of his truck and took me to the Medicine Woman. While she performed the drawing out of poison and the healing, he cooked the snake over a fire and ate it while the rattle was cleaned of its meat on an ant-hill. "Ants work fast." he said as he held a leather strap with the rattle tied to it, and I hung it around my neck.

As we were leaving the trailer, a man was at the door just about to knock. "Hi," he said nervously as we walked out, "I'm looking for my brother. He came out here from L.A. a while ago and I haven't heard from him since." He went on to describe his brother, his hair and height and face.

"Oh yeah, I haven't seen him in a long time." Jackrabbit replied, ejecting the man with a casual, detached tone. In the truck, Jackrabbit turned the key, the engine roared, and he said, "He's never gonna find that guy." I waited silently for more. "He came out here from Los Angeles, told us all he was holding up away from trouble at home. He was bad news, man. Wasn't long before he started takin' advantage of people, and we gave him fair warning. The cops don't come around here, we got our own law. You be good to people and they'll be good to you, but don't fuck with us, man. Keep doing wrong here and no one'll ever see you again. We dropped that fucker headfirst down a mineshaft."

He knew exactly where my car was without any word from me. There it sat, untouched. I thanked him as I stepped out. He pointed to a dirt track and said it was a good road. There were no diverging trails and it was the best way to get where I was going. Before I closed the door, he said, "See ya later, Rattlesnake."

I was compelled by his advice, and also had the strange feeling he would see which way I went. It led me through the hills into raw, vast desert. I stopped and got out, gazing, breathing, and my eyes were caught by the burned-out skeleton of a car and, not far from it, was a dark hole in the ground.

In the Locker

Been adrift so long
out of time or thought.
An eternity he's been lost,
though he's not quite sure,
could've been only an hour or so.
The boat went down fast.
Ever since,
he's been in this tiny raft,
able to see nothing
through the dense fog.
So hot, skin burning,
and the water too warm
to cool him.
The air is low, heavy,
stagnant.
No breeze, no sound.
He drank the last of his
fresh water.
Did he ever have any at all?
Too hot to think,
too hungry and thirsty,
too lonely.
Night hasn't fallen in ages,
seems it never will.
What's that?
A rope!
Was that always there?
Extending from the hull,
out into the water
and vanishing into the fog.
Grabbing the rope
with his last hope,
he tugs and yanks,
but the line is ungiving
and the raft will not budge.

He's had enough now
and dives in
to follow the length of the cord,
swimming in the motionless sea.
Something there,
a shape ahead.
There,
his raft?
Yes, though he kept a straight course.
Confused, exhausted, angry,
he closes his eyes
and expels air to let himself sink.
And needing breath badly,
he doesn't care to rise.
Anything at all
he might see before drowning,
he wondered, even a speck
against the void
would give some ease at his end.
At the last moment,
before his lungs revolt in pain,
he flings his eyelids open wide.
Suddenly, he is dry,
sitting in the raft,
shrouded in heavy fog.

Never a Dull Day

Gertrude awoke before sunrise to prepare breakfast for her family and was already sitting on the porch with a cup of coffee when her husband woke up. As the dawn's mist began to dissipate, Sam shuffled out to sit with his wife and saw her wrapped up to her shoulders in a big blanket, the steam from her mug rising in front of her snout, the most beautiful creature he had ever seen. When she smiled at him, he understood why humans used the saying that their heart was bursting out of their chest, though for him it was like someone had poured fresh, clean mud all over his heart and life was perfect.

"Good morning, big boar." She always started the day teasing him.

"Good morning, my love." Sam smiled and they rubbed their snouts together. He sat down next to her and knew she could smell the whisky in his coffee. This would be a hard day on the farm. They hadn't finished expanding the fences, but they'd have to make do. The humans needed to be brought in from pasture.

After his coffee, Sam hustled down the steps to get started. Gertrude loved the sound of his hooves as they clopped off the porch in the morning. She loved seeing him ride out on horseback in his flannel and jeans. She heard a squeal from one of her piglets in the house and thumping sounds accompanying their own little cloppity hooves, then more squealing and laughing. She went inside to clean up breakfast and help them get dressed and ready for school in the parlor. Today, each at their little desks, she would teach them math and writing and tell them stories.

Sam sat atop his horse, rolling his eyes and aggravated while trying to ride slowly so he didn't trample the humans. Every time he had to move them from one place to another, they would swarm around his horse talking about their problems and their wants and their opinions and their beliefs and their questions and their needs and their arguments and their love. Ugh, they were obnoxious. Ranching cattle was much simpler. They just did their thing. They knew what they needed. Even when they were stubborn or playful and ran off to explore, they knew where their home was. He missed those animals. These humans did almost nothing but argue with each other. It was a wretched duty, but someone had to do it. Someone had to keep them contained.

It was a long day. He missed his wife and he couldn't wait to get home. Her grace was what kept up his humor, that and his rowdy piglets. One of the humans broke away yelling, I'm freeeee! Sam breathed a sigh, "Damnit." He rode around the young man and shouted, but this was a particularly stubborn one and wouldn't go back. Sam used to try reasoning with them, but it was pointless. Now, he just lassoed and hurried them to the herd. This will be much easier, he thought, when my piggies are old enough to help. Hopefully by then, though, I'll have cattle again, or sheep. Anything but humans.

Once he got the young man back, a few more began anxiously shoving each other. Yelling obscenities, an older man ran off and tried to punch Sam's horse as he was being wrangled. The horse reared up and Sam fell off, landing on a sharp rock shoulder-first. The rest of the afternoon, he tried to drive them while dragging the runners back, and his bruised shoulder tightened up. Once, he lassoed two at a time and when he brought them in, they began growling and hitting each other. He didn't understand these animals. No one did. The important thing was that they were cared for, restrained from causing a ruckus all over the world, fed daily and allowed to roam in the pasture, just enough freedom so they wouldn't rebel.

Later, after dinner and under the blue and orange sunset sky, Sam and Gertrude sat on the porch. She laid a blanket over their laps and her head on his shoulder while an ice pack cooled the other he'd fallen on. The empty fenced-in field of the morning was now full of humans moseying around, mumbling in ever-changing groups. "Ah, I don't like that." Sam said.

"What?"

"It looks like they're forming herds within herds. It's weird."

"Oh, I wouldn't worry. You've wrangled stronger animals than those."

"I shouldn't have sold the cattle. I know it was necessary, but I'm so sick of herding humans. They're stupid and they stink."

"I know, honey. Maybe next season we can look into slowly transitioning back to cattle. We just have to figure out how to make it work financially."

"Yeah."

A howl went up from the field and then the entire herd was yelling and fighting. There was a loud crack as part of the fence broke and the unruly humans poured out of the enclosure, fleeing and shouting. Sam cussed and jumped up, Gertrude yelled into the house telling the children to stay inside, and together on horseback they rode into the sunset. Never a dull day on a pig farm.

The Doctor

In his white coat
He paces the house
Up the staircase
Through the hall
In and out
Of the doors
Save one door
Which remains nailed shut
Behind it is his wife
She's been sleeping
Two years
She should be up soon
And the cat
Out in the yard
Has been napping
Under the same bush
For months
Lazy creature
Shadow claws at the doctor
In the dim light
The fireplace keeps him safe
Or so he believes
And he never looks in the mirror
Not anymore
He's scared of his face

The Right Words

Giogor stood alone in the dark at the locked gate of the marina. His wife and two young daughters entered earlier in the day while the gate was open. But now a password was required, a puzzle specific to each person trying to enter. He could see the ship rocking in the water where they were waiting for him, huddled with the others, hoping he made it in time. He impatiently tapped the gun at his side, but knew that force was useless. If he fired, the lock would seal itself and the ships would leave.

He was thankful to be the last one. If there'd been a mob of other escapees needing to get through, he wouldn't be able to concentrate. *You'd think they'd unlock the gate for a mass evacuation.* But the government of Dên had never really cared about the people it claimed to govern. Why else would they have escaped with the military while the Tayrshon invaded? Now, he and those who remained were taking the last undrowned ships to another planet.

The wheeled mechanism on the gate turned and folded in and out of itself with each correct answer from its would-be opener. [What is your family's name?] After a few tries, he stopped answering "Yandas" and remembered something his grandmother always said, something he told his girls. "We are the ones, the ones who came before any others, before the Terran and before the Tayrshon. We are the ones who belong here." Unsure, Giogor answered "the ones" and the lock clicked and turned, changing its configuration and asking another question. [Who are you?] He immediately thought of his daughters. "A father," he answered and the lock changed again, preparing a new question.

He'd gone back for the sigil his grandmother wore before she succumbed to the Tayrshon poison. Now, he wondered if he should have just left it. The ships would be leaving soon, with or without him. But no, the sigil was proof that they're the ones who were here before. The sigil which now hung on his neck would remind his family for generations of where they came from, no matter what planet they went to for safety.

"Hey," a kindly voice behind him intruded, "think you're getting through?"

Giogor turned and saw a Terran man approaching. "Yeah, I'm on the last question." He turned back to listen as the puzzle toned. [It doesn't matter.]

The man behind him stated the obvious, "What? That's not a question."

These fucking locks.

"What does it mean, 'It doesn't matter'? Last time I went through, the questions weren't as hard as that."

Giogor was trying to think, trying not to panic.

"Are you sure this is your last question?"

"Yes."

"Other people have to get through too, you know. Did your family get away, already?"

I'm gonna knock this guy's teeth out.

"How long before the ships just leave us?"

"Do you want to get through or not? The Tayrshon are almost here."

"Not almost."

Fuck. Giogor turned and saw the man slowly ripping his skin off. Underneath was the black face and pinpoint eyes of a Tayrshon. It tore away another strip of skin and hissed through its sharp teeth, "Just relax. It doesn't hurt." Giogor reached for his gun, but a long limb shot out of the false ribs and gripped his hand tight to the holster. "Ah ah ah, no need. Just relax."

"Alright, hold on. Let me take this off." The Tayrshon were used to last requests, especially this one from Giogor's species. The hosts would slowly fade away after they were poisoned, but their image would be worn by the invaders. Terran almost always yelled and fought to the death or cowered in fear, but the natives of Dên were calmer, better equipped to accept the inevitable, and simply did not want to dishonor their sigils by having them worn by their murderers.

With his free hand, Giogor pulled the sigil's cord over his head and lowered it to the ground, then swung it and struck the invader's face. The creature's grip on his holster released and he shot the Tayrshon as many times as it took for him to believe it was dead.

Now, back to the lock. He needed to find the right words. The ships would be leaving soon, skirting on the water before ascending into space toward whichever planet had been assigned. *It doesn't matter*, he thought, *that's not a question... Exactly, it's not a question.* "Does it matter?" he asked. The lock remained silent. It never repeated the puzzle. It only waited for the right words.

Giogor heard rustling behind him and shot the fake Terran now standing again. But at his feet still laid the creature he killed, and above it was the identical man whose image it had taken. Giogor grabbed him as he fell, the blast in his gut pulsing blood.

"Did he get you?" the Terran asked in short breaths, "I was following him so he wouldn't get anyone else."

"No, he didn't get me."

"Good. Get through the gate and go somewhere better."

Somewhere better. The Terran were always looking for new places. Dên was Giogor's home, it was a good place. Terrans couldn't see it the way he did. He pitied their dissatisfaction, but they were a good people when they wanted to be. "I'm so sorry."

"I'll be dead from the poison soon, anyway. It doesn't matter."

"Yes, it does."

With those words, the lock clicked, turned, and the gate opened.

He Rode Out To Join The Fray

There was a Cruithne warrior
and he rode out to join the fray,
but left his heart at home with her
till his return at end of day.

The Romans had been at their throats,
so he rode out to join the fray.
He swore that he would burn their boats
and then return at end of day.

His clan saw legionnaires pass by
when they rode out to join the fray.
They howled with rage their battlecry
and fought until the end of day.

The lady waited for her love
as he rode out to join the fray,
but saw no omen from above
that he'd return at end of day.

Then came sounds of marching feet,
those who rode out to join the fray.
Her heart did leap and skip a beat
to see him at the end of day.

But, these men had not come to save
when they rode out to join the fray.
Those Romans took her as a slave
to weep until the end of day.

The warrior lay awaiting death,
for he rode out to join the fray.
He spoke her name with one last breath
and ne'er returned at end of day.

The Blobs

-squat, round, fleshy blobs. What used to be hands were now fleshy pads to hold their screens, with one appendage to wrap around and flick the screen to motion, to which their attention was unflinchingly shackled. Information was absorbed and excreted moment to moment. The square wooden pallets upon which they sat had long since broken down at the wheels, with no need to move, as all survival and entertainment was inducted into their veins. Inventions to implant screens into their eyes had not been necessary by the time they were developed. They all watched and relayed a video of an asteroid colliding with the moon. One was watching, and then its pallet cracked and broke its final inch to the ground. It was jolted to an unexpected position and saw the moon still there in the daylight sky, unbroken, serene, and realized no one knew. They did not think of looking for themselves. They'd already seen it on their screens and discussed the theoretical effects of a shattered moon, having taken this news as presented, and made it part of their culture. This one, now dipped crooked on the ground, looked around and saw aisles of pink pallet-sitters, blobs unmoving. Is this what we are? It thought. It tried to call out, though its voice from lack of use was untouchable, and having silently relayed certain combinations of words for so long it forgot how to say anything from its own mind. It noticed the one sitting nearest was not the one it had always seen as nearest in video-picture communications. It barely knew this one. It sat, staring at the rows and rows of blobs with their heads tilted down. It was a long time before it thought to add to the screen-stories what it had seen. It found it could not move its appendage, for its muscles cramped and its skin had grown over the device. The best picture possible would have to suffice. The click of the camera sent into the static air a photo of the grey, flat, cement field where they lived, bored and entertained. It tried again to move and was able to send another picture, one of the full watching moon. It could feel the invisible pulse when each saw it, one by one affected, though unmoving, a healthy skip of the heart. Unable at this new angle on its broken pallet to turn its neck and look at the screen for long, it watched the blobs, it watched the moon, clearness of the sky it had forgotten, and the night and day which fluctuated more regularly than it had known. Eventually, the pictures passed out of memory as all pictures did and sustenance came less and less through the tube in its vein as it flicked at the screen less and less. Then the sustenance stopped, having received no feedback from what it calculated was an outdated lifeform. It was around this time the blob, nearly dead from lack of nutrition, saw a head in the crowd stiffly and somewhat painfully look up from its screen.

In the valley

Ingvar held back tears as his brother Kar confessed his plan to leave. No one went willingly to the valley, for it meant death, and not a soft death. To creep through the dark twisting tunnels of the lost cave only for a chance to reach the terrors on the other side, this was proof of total despair. Kar was indeed consumed by despair and dishonor. No amount of pleading from his brother could alter his decision.

It didn't matter to the rest of the tribe that it was an accident. They were good friends and they were only playing near the cliffs. Upon seeing her son's shattered corpse, the boy's mother rose in madness and demanded retribution. Murder meant punishment by being struck with a stone from each person in the tribe. And if you survived, exile.

They dwelled in a harsh place of death and starvation. There were stories of other tribes across the land, but no living generation had ever seen an outsider. They were the only people in the world, except those who lived in the valley. The valley, full and green and bountiful, but not a place to live. It could not be found over the land. The only way to reach it was through the lost cave.

Ingvar heard the tribe approaching.

"We're here to take your brother."

"You can find him in the valley."

There was a hushed pause. "Do you really expect us to believe you? Tell us where he is or we'll hunt him down ourselves."

"Go hunt, then!"

They searched and searched, but never found Kar. Still, they could hardly trust that he'd gone to the valley willingly. Anyone else, anyone, would have chosen death by their family's thrown stones than to take that course. Whatever it was, they knew not the cause. That place just did horrid things to people. It twisted their minds. Sometimes, when the air was still and their desolate home was eerily silent, someone might say they heard screams echoing from the lost cave. The screaming of the lost people. Lost in their minds.

After finding no fugitive, the tribe would only pass Ingvar with sharp glances, cursing his brother's name. He thought that perhaps Kar's escape was best, that maybe his rush to the valley was a better alternative. These people didn't deserve their revenge. But, those were just fleeting notions. Ingvar had to save his brother from that place. Better dead than lost. He believed he could bring him safely home before the insanity seeped in, but only if he went without delay. He could keep Kar hidden underground in his own cavernous dwelling. The dead boy's hateful mother would never give Kar sincere forgiveness. So a gloomy, dragging life it would be, but he would be alive, if only in secrecy. Ingvar ran, unafraid of what horrors he might encounter. His brother was in danger. That was his only concern. All the quarrels these siblings ever had were meaningless now, unless to draw them closer together. What is more important than the real and lasting bond?

The entrance was just across from their clustered hillside caves, always in sight. Children were warned from their youngest years to stay away, for even straying too close might get one caught in its strange pull. There was a story about one of the tribe's strongest and bravest ancestors who wanted to free his people from that wretched hole. First, he trekked for years, but found no place to sustain them. So upon returning, he decided to close the cavern by piling stones so large and heavy that only he could budge them. After the first big boulder was in place, a single one which he rolled up the hill on his own, he succumbed to the gravity of the other side. And that rock still sat beside the entrance, where the mightiest of men sat for only a moment before being drawn in.

For courage, Ingvar gathered into his gut all the rage from every pain he ever endured and the ones he hadn't endured very well. He would need the strength of his rage to carry any real hope of making it through. He would not allow the tenderness of hopeful prayers, for with them come the worries of hopelessness. He had to bury any gentleness deep and concealed so it could not turn against him and ruin what he had to do.

Into the cave he went. The sunlight reaching into the first stretching hunchway soon darkened to absolute blackness as the tunnel curved and cornered. He slowly made his way with one hand on the rocky walls. Time creeps differently underground and there is no direction through endless changes of the earth. Far within and frustrated by the impenetrable dark, Ingvar slumped down on his knees, but almost the same moment he stood up again. He couldn't stop. Around another turn, he heard a faint, rushing sound. His audible guide grew louder. Never had he heard such a continuous noise, but it was comforting in a way. Then, it was so loud he could not discern where it was coming from. Trying one way, the sound quieted, so he went back around another curve in the darkness and the sound was louder again, then another turn and louder.

He hooted in joy, though he couldn't hear himself through the roaring. There was light, dim and rippling on the cave walls. Moving faster around one final turn, he was struck by the sight of water falling in a heavy curtain, daylight shining through. Cool air blew in with a thick mist. Ingvar was amazed at what looked like rain as thick as a stone. He cupped his hands and drank, and drank, and drank. A few moments showed him more water than he'd ever seen in his entire life. He held his head in, letting it wash over him, then stepped back and ran through it, falling a short drop into a shallow pool.

Standing in the cold water, he could barely breathe looking at the valley around him. He sobbed as desperately as an honest child. Ingvar tried to ration his sight. It was too much. He stepped dripping wet out of the pool. It was a thriving forest between towering grey cliffs, the sun soaring directly overhead through a misty green canopy where birds chirped and swooned among the tall, silent trees.

He wouldn't let Kar slip from his mind, but there was an overwhelming sense of living energy. The water into which Ingvar had fallen was but one single link in a long chain of shimmering pools coursing like liquid diamonds. If the tribe knew how it really was on the other side, they would all trade their sanity to stay here forever. Though a very short forever it would be.

He climbed up a high rock to scout the area, but the only movement he could discern was caused by the breeze. He searched on foot at a slow run, then halting, creeping, running, halting, creeping, continuing cautiously through the pathless wildland. He heard a voice? Probably a bird. Two steps and he heard it again, definitely a voice. A small voice. He tracked it around a boulder and his gut fell at the sight of a young boy with his fingertips in his mouth, mumbling. Ingvar reached out to the boy, but pulled back before laying a hand on his shoulder. There was something wrong with this, more than he could see. He backed away quietly.

There was a crashing sound and he ran toward it. Kar emerged bloody and scraped from thorny bushes. Ingvar grabbed his brother and pulled him close, but Kar pushed away. "Get away from me! I'm not going back!"

"Look at yourself."

A disturbed, savage howl shook their bones. "Go home." Kar said as he fled. Ingvar saw the free choice, the other side, and understood it was best. Going back to hide in a cave would mean a slow, pointless wasting away in misery. At least in the valley he could live guiltless under the sun, however briefly.

Deciding to find his way back, he went first to the sound of the river and drank from it. As he walked along its course, there was nothing familiar. Refusing to stray from the waterside, he recognized his surroundings less and less. Fright came fast upon him. A massive boulder half on land and half in the water damned a pond behind it that emptied in an easy torrent. He kept his hand on the rock to move around it and get back in sight of the river.

He was frozen stiff as he reached the pond and his eyes found pale legs, hips, breasts, and a piercing face surrounded by long hair. She noticed him. The sun was setting. As she walked slowly toward him from the water, the low orange light set her body glistening. He was trapped in wonder. The night was long and when their embrace was over, Ingvar fell into a heavy, blank sleep.

When he awoke, the woman was gone and he'd been in the valley far too long. He was closed in by flat walls of reddish-grey. The ground was covered in a layer of loose grey snow, like ash to the touch and not cold. It was dark, with a strange cast of dim light. Stretching ahead of him was a cramped, low corridor. On hands and knees he crawled.

To Learn of Giving

There was a hermit who lived by the river collecting nuts and berries while strolling leisurely among the trees.

One day, a man came stumbling near his hut where the hermit was chopping wood. He begged for money, but the hermit had none. He did have fish he'd caught that morning, and soon they were eating by the fire and sharing a pot of tea. They remained at the hearth late into the night and the hermit sang a few songs on his guitar. He could see the man was tired and offered him a place to sleep.

The man was still asleep when the hermit awoke in the morning and went for a stroll. When he returned, the man and the guitar were gone.

The season passed and the hermit stood in his doorway, wrapped in a blanket, looking out at the glittering snow. Suddenly, he saw that same man approaching timidly, wearing rags and shivering. He did not see the hermit until he reached the hut and immediately rattled apologies and excuses faster than the hermit wanted to keep up. He wrapped the man in the blanket and brought him inside where the warm air stung and healed him.

Morning came and the hermit awoke on the floor. He looked to his bed where the guest had slept, which was empty of man and blanket. He went to prepare a morning meal, but when he opened the wooden crate where he kept his food, it was empty.

The hermit's living continued peacefully and spring arose on the river. While tilling the garden with his bare hands, shouts abruptly shattered the silence and he recognized that man's voice, among others. As the man neared the hut, he was struck down by three burly men. "Help me!" he yelled as two of the men bound him with rope and dragged him away. Another politely apologized for the disturbance. "We caught him stealing from our village." The hermit returned to tilling his garden and never saw the man again.

Primordial

Sunrise in the wilderness
the tribe rises to dance.
Up from the earth to lead in step
Cernunnos, Lord of the Wild.

Around the Tree of Life
clans of free and happy folk
and the spirit with antlers seven-tined
live in the primal forest.

Here come two new lovers sweet
enraptured full and amorous
in torrid embrace beneath the Tree
intense in high passion.

The games and silly songs
of playful children laughing
who feel the world's imagination
and brightly colored dreams.

Crack! In the woods.
What could it be?
Then enter demons
who burn and defile.

The strangers have no faces
only dark masks and cold
suits standing stiff in droves
and staring blank, unfeeling.

The children run afraid
and the sharp fire advances
the sound like rusting machines
in rolling, grinding malice.

They chop and hack at the Great Tree
and the limbs are severed and sent
leaving the once-mighty ancestor
in a tortured pile of ruin.

With the industrians gone from the wreck
the Horned One and children return
and weep over the death
and the tribe is called together.

Warriors shout and don their bodies
with muddy hunting paint
and dance their furious battlecries
of stomping, howling, beating breasts.

They go, those fearsome men, to fight
to kill the slayers of the land
to rid the world of this death
and save their home from dread.

Away in the factory, dead-cold and dusty
the civilized gather the remains
shaping, stamping, wiring the wood
to form new soldiers and pawns.

The assimilated ranks of drones
are sent away to their tasks
and the crafty engineers
make a spectacle.

Not quite a dance, but some strange rite
the faceless slither and crawl
from open mouths ensues dark sludge
vomiting asphalt on the ground.

They revel in it shamelessly
rubbing themselves with toxic slime
while the warriors on a hilltop
watch in disgust.

Shouting, they brave the sticky mire
and clash with cyborg soldiers
but the tools under tired influence
flee for their synthetic skin.

The robotic ranks marching
come upon the women of the tribe
bringing with them a gilded cage
with glittering bars and glowing lights.

In phalanx conformity
they display their perfection
gesturing politely to their customers
and ushering them into the cell.

Signs are shining bright
pointing with many lies
flashing with words oddly luring-
Beauty, Wealth, Freedom.

In, the fooled mothers go
and the door is slammed shut
while they weep and yell
calling for their young ones.

They are taken
to be raped and torn
and the children wander helplessly
awaiting the sight of their fathers.

Soon the young are snared and bound tight
crying as they are beaten
and with chains and heavy locks
the slavers drive the children.

They are whipped when they cry
and taken to a steaming shop
held by the neck to sweat
working over assembly lines.

One breaks loose
and aids the others
in making the workhouse
chaos and flames.

No exit to be found, though
escaping the angered gears
and they fall into the merciless grips
their necks broken with a twist.

The rogue-fire hissing is extinguished
and the cleaners see the approaching
fathers who find their dead children
and thus the battle begins.

The plastic vultures swarm
the wild, screaming men
and cut them apart
like firewood.

Cernunnos appears
and is alive to fight.
Yet, he too is overwhelmed
and trampled into the ground.

Victory march of industrial splendor
briefcases flinging wide
issuing smoke and cash
flying into the air.

In a short-lived moment
they are bent and sick and sluggish
gasping for breath
and falling to the ground.

Quietly
the earth regains
uplifting the massacred bodies
where rises the Tree of Life.

The Red Man Desert

Derry was a town named after the same place in Ireland, but it was as far from a green-grassed riverbank as it could be. The people who lived there were hard and cruel and the land was worse. Its dry air was filled with dust and the miners carried themselves as if they were already dead. One business ruled their lives and one businessman, Mr. Cane, like the kind of cane nuns wielded to discipline children. He owned the coal mines, the general store, and the miners' tents were rented from him in a direct line of cash from himself to himself. He had in his employ a small army of paid guards and nowhere could a man walk freely. The dead-men miners were ignored while spied on as if living in a prison. There was nothing they could do but sleep and drink whiskey and eat from their batches of rations bought with blood and sweat and sometimes death in the ground which they entered before sunrise and exited after sunset, never seeing the sun except on its official day.

It was one of these Sundays that John walked into the dirt road, eating a sliver of meat, sauntering like he would never know a better moment than filling his mouth with something that tasted vaguely like home. The cooking fire's smoke drifted across his face and stung his eyes, but it was a sweet sting.

He heard a high-pitched shout like a lightning bolt in his spine and it jarred him to a stop. A line of feather-headed horse-mounted warriors stared at him from the top of the hill, the yellow-orange sunset blazing behind their backs. Mr. Cane and his men scattered out of their wooden barracks and began firing. Their guns were as useless as if the stocks crumbled apart in their hands. Not a single warrior was harmed, and the dust attacked Mr. Cane's men as swiftly as spears and clubs. An arrow skittered past John in the dirt. He thought it might have been his hunger, the hunger which always lasted after he'd eaten at the end of a long day, as he chuckled and realized why they were called "braves". He didn't need to look behind him to know his fellow miners were watching, unmoving. From their heat-splintered wooden tables, some with mouths wide open waiting for food which may never reach them, some chugging warm whiskey and apologizing to their mommas, they were an audience to the slaughter and felt no urgency when the army of guards yelled for their help.

Bloody mud splattered on John's face when a warrior on horseback approached him. He was restful in the thought that his head would be struck by a quick club, but nearly fainted when the red man spoke softly. John had no answer to the strange language. The man turned to his band and as they talked, he realized they were not the monsters he'd been told. In their eyes was the same interested concern of boys watching frogs seem to speak in their turn by the stream. Then, one of them reached out with a woven blanket. John took it and bowed and felt silly. The red men trod off in silence and returned to the desert.

A Curse

He stalked the night forest, the moon's pale light scarcely penetrating the trees with leaves of pure shadow. These were the woods where no one goes. No trails, but many gruesome tales.

That day, the weather had been somber, holding a hush over the village and the road that passed along nearby. Even the men and birds in the fields were silent, when any other day they'd be singing and whistling happy tunes. Many found themselves doing nothing at all but sitting in the soft grey daylight, a few on haystacks smoking their pipes, silently filling and refilling mugs from a large bottle of honey whisky. It was a quiet day, with nothing more unusual than a reserved laziness upon the folk.

Jeremiah was already more reserved than any boy his age. The atmosphere suited his solitary temperament. He rushed to finish his chores and disappeared before he could be caught with inquiries from his parents. They would, if they knew, put a stop to his frequent travels in the woods.

There was only a short path of grass between his family's cornfield and the edge of the forbidden trees, and it was too easy for him to escape unseen. He felt at home here and nowhere else, and though he could never question it openly, he couldn't understand why the town despised this place. Some of their haunting tales were so terrifying that the actual events were left unsaid and purposely forgotten by long dead grandparents, leaving their progeny with obscure warnings. "I told you not to go near the woods. Remember the girl who never came home?" and that was as much as the children and parent-children knew, that long ago a girl went into the woods and never returned. "How many times have I told you not to gather firewood near those trees? You'll wish you had listened when you end up with the curse." and what the curse was, no one knew.

None of it ever frightened Jeremiah. None in the

village were like him. And so he didn't speak of it. At times, he wondered if it was the curse, but then he'd run to the trees and feel like he was home, not cursed. When he watched the neighboring pack of wolves from high up in the branches, he felt no fear, only an unpronounceable kinship.

The last of the day's cloud cover had passed away with the sunset. The full moon was rising higher and Jeremiah knew he was lost in the dark, shifting forest, but he had no desire to leave. He had a strange sense in his nostrils. He didn't know it in words, but he grasped it in his jaws and eyes and ears.

He came to a clearing out of the heavy canopy where a single tree stood on a grassy hillock. Stepping out, uncomfortably vulnerable in the open space, he made his way to the tree. There, he could see the isolated moonlit meadow encircled by black woods which when night fell spread to cover the entire world, then shrank back at sunrise to its own daunting space.

He lingered there and was suddenly caught by the gaze of a giant wolf. Beautiful. He stared a moment and then heard a deep growling behind him. Before he turned his head, he felt the crush of teeth on his leg. The two wolves attacked, then another and another. They ruthlessly tore his young body to shreds.

Crying out, his voice changed its tone from tragic wrenching pain to a burst of howling that raised the ground in shivers. The wolves leapt back, crouching and straining side to side. Jeremiah writhed and howled, feeling his bones pounded with sledgehammers. But he also felt himself grow every bit as strong. Compared to this, the ripping teeth of wolves were like papercuts.

He regained a different composure and then swung and flailed madly at the wolves. His limbs were heavy as the lower branches of an ancient oak, with more than enough power to give a savage, endless beating. He towered over his attackers and grabbed one's head in his huge, bestial claws. Then, his gaping mouth dropped like an anvil into his prey.

The remainder of the pack drifted away from the madness, limping and bleeding. Jeremiah's bloody howls rumbled the stars and awakened slumbering ghosts.

Morning, the village was in a tearful search. His mother sat in her chair since his absence, then lifted her head and looked out the window with sudden knowing and ran through the cornfield, into the forest, calling her son's name with a voice cracking in despair.

The creature woke to the noise and soon found the frantic caller, but he was far from recognizing his own name. From behind the trees he watched her searching and began to feel hungry.

Zombie Dream

They were gathered in the brick-walled compound, some being bandaged, some sitting in the sunshine by the pool as if there weren't hordes of zombies trying to find an unguarded space to break through. He silently cursed himself. In the skirmish this morning, he chased a howling straggler across the tiled roofs. As he laid into it with a shotgun, the rogue gnashing teeth of another caught his arm.

He told no one. They congratulated him on the kill and didn't notice the bite. He took his shotgun and walked off alone, watching them in their happy momentary protection. *Damn it*, he thought, the unspeakable irritation of slipping up what could have been escaped. But watching the joy bought with bravery, the peace of the inevitable was coming upon him.

Not yet. He kept a strict vigil for any emergency or mischance. In case anyone in the world might need his help, he would be ready. His eyesight became blurry and bright and his mind slowed, taking on a new clarity. He felt an overwhelming knowledge that all is right.

Watching: a toddler about to trip headfirst laughing into the water. He began to reach out as the mother turned around and picked up her child, smiling. Watching: a young boy drowning? No. Holding his breath, he splashed up with a playful gasp of air. Watching: flesh-eating corpses climbing over the barbed-wire? No. A few men reinforcing the barriers with higher coils to catch the zombies and shoot them dead-again.

Everywhere he turned was the beginning of something needing his attention, but everywhere he turned was taken care of before he could reach. His presence was waning. The need for his life was coming to completion. He wanted to be useful. He had the will to stand and watch as long as he could, to make sure they had all they needed. And they did. He was happy to know. He had one final duty to undertake. He watched a moment longer and smiled seeing them all together, keeping each other safe. Living. He walked around the farthest corner and out of the compound with the shotgun over his shoulder, and no one heard the blast of it, but he let himself out as politely as he could.

Harmonica

She walked through the garden and heard a small whistling sound that sputtered through the jasmine vines. She wondered what it was and might've asked the ravens on a branch above her, but they were singing in the apple tree and wouldn't have heard what it was. This garden was her and she was this garden, and hearing a new, unknown sound was as strange to her as suddenly growing a new limb. The fae do not bend their whim to the circumstances. Their power is that of pure will and pure joy. And so she sought it out, this almost-music, to befriend it or cast it out of her realm.

A man, leaving the conversation which bored him at a tea party with white dresses and proper manners where he felt like a tangle-haired sap-smelling wild boy, sat on a stone bench in an alcove of the hedge maze where the jasmine hadn't been tended in ages. The old lady of the house had called for her favorite garden game, *Find The Apple Tree.* Though the lady swore with sincerity that the tree really did exist, no one had ever found it. The search through the maze would inevitably slow as guests found themselves wandering and engaging in mingled talk, and they assumed this was part of the game and the way it was meant to be ended. And so, the man found his way to this place, having glimpsed hidden light through the vines.

Pushing his way through spiderwebs while flowers dropped in his hair, he realized this place must have been ignored just long enough for the gardeners to think it was part of the hedge. He was secluded, where he'd always belonged, since he really was a tangle-haired sap-smelling boy who ran away from the orphanage. They weren't cruel, but they were strict and he was alone, not alone as he was now in the happiness of quiet solitude, but alone as a child with a wild heart and parents who were missing. He was told by the nuns that they found him as a baby outside their gate, wrapped in a strange cloth with a leafy branch upon him.

They told him to be grateful and that his mother surely made the best decision she could. He was grateful to the nuns, but he belonged with the trees and the stars. He could feel it. One night, he snuck out through the bars surrounding the orphanage and escaped into the forest.

There, he lived comfortably and happily. He was content for uncountable years, so long he could speak with every animal and was friends with many generations of their families. He knew every part of the woods from the treetops to the stones and every burrow underground. The forest was always new and always home. But eventually, he felt the call for a change of adventure. Making his way to the narrow road where wagons sometimes travelled, he waited until he saw someone who looked like a good, kind soul. The trader with his wagon full of goods was surprised to see a young man appear from the bushes like a wolf. He offered him food and warm red wine and gave him a blanket to wrap himself in.

Countable years went by after that, though he didn't care to count them, until at last he found his way through work and through learning to this garden party of tea and white dresses. The game had indeed become walking conversations and he escaped from the monotony. Beside him on the stone bench was a rusty harmonica, still seeming to have plenty of lively enthusiasm in it. The last time it was played must have been when the old lady of the house was a little girl. He put it gently to his mouth and blew an odd tune.

Suddenly, he noticed a grassy mound and the top of an ancient stump. He wondered if that was where the apple tree once had been. Then he kept playing, quietly so no one would hear.

As the faery woman neared the sound, a feeling of familiarity began to enliven her spirit. A misty, reddish figure appeared on the garden bench.

The man thought he saw the shape of a woman, but as soon as he looked, the shape disappeared as if it hadn't been there at all. It felt strange, and he went back to playing.

The woman saw leaves and flowers in his hair as the figure on the bench became clearer.

A scent reached the man through the rust of his breath, and it was somehow a scent he had always known. In a moment, ravens sang and red apples danced on branches above where the stump had been. They were bright as if each one was a sun and when his eyes adjusted to their light, he could see the shape and face of a woman smiling at him and crying. Her face looked like his and she felt like home.

She watched him appear with the music and at once knew the face of her son, the infant she sent to the mortal world.

Not much was made of his disappearance, for he was well-liked, but not well-known. Generations would pass who never found the apple tree in the old lady's garden. But, when one day her descendant found an unseen alcove while playing hide-and-seek, she discovered within it the statue of a man sitting on a stone bench playing harmonica.

Rats in the Wreckage

Out from the shore
marooned on a sandbar
sits a wrecked ship-
the Dart.
For a long time it's been
rotting and rusting
and upon it lives a company of rats.
Here comes the ol' fat marshal now
with his fancy cane and greasy fur.
'Tis he who oversees all operations
of the colony
demanding more refuse collected
during the nights of diligent scavenging.
Yet it seems for the bilge-rats
though they work ever harder
there is never enough for all.
They've seen how the marshal
and his board of accomplices
budget for great treats
from the communal rations
and it shows
while the rodent mass caste
is sentenced to a decreased portion
of the food they gathered themselves.
Not nearly enough to survive.
What can be said by the serfs
while those few flaunt their luxury?
Those who've spoken
against the greed and theft
are made an example
and are soon found dead.
Now, this wrecked ship
was slowly tipping toward the sea
as the rats guessed
but knew not for certain.

The marshal, however,
he kept track
and he knew it was going under.
But, as is common
of the self-concerned
he did not use his knowledge
for the best of all.
Instead, the ship ran stricter
with more demanded and less given
while he took more for himself
and a few crony crooks,
so when the Dart
finally fell too far
they alone would have food
and fine things
and the workers
would be left with nothing.
But, Nature has ways
of punishing selfishness...
When the night was upon them
and the ship to be abandoned
those few big gluttons
guarded their horde
and fought off those who had earned it
and who only ever asked for a mouthful.
Eventually, they turned in hunger
and swam to the shore
to sunshine and a new life
a chance to live on their own free terms.
And the marshal with his cruel posse
remained with their heavy wealth.
Never could they leave their robbed riches
and never could they swim with the weight.
The others reached the beach
just as the sun was rising
and they watched the Dart
fall into the sea with a splash.

It sank and disappeared
and the selfish ones drowned
in their greed.

A Hamburger For A Hero

Tommy stood by the table full of food hoping no one talked to him, hoping he could remain invisible. Why did he let himself be dragged to this party? As soon as they walked in, his friend disappeared to flirt with Amelia even though he knew Tommy was in love with her. He could have been at home playing the new video game he just bought. Now, he was just the fat kid eating a hamburger by himself.

The apartment smelled like the crunchy socks of whoever lived there, or whoever slept on the couch every night and refused to shower. It was loud, too loud to hear why anyone was having fun. They might have been here for New Year's Eve, but midnight would come and go without anybody noticing. Couples would be fighting, idiots would be wrestling and breaking the beer-pong table, stoners would be half asleep and talking about plans they would forget before morning, all while they should have been kissing and falling in love or at home playing video games.

Amelia had liked Tommy enough to tell him, but weeks went by and he was too scared to call her. She was so pretty; part of him didn't believe she could actually like him. Traumatized by middle and high school pranks, the most likely scenario was that this was another joke. The small place in his mind that thought she really did like him was also afraid of getting his ass kicked again. The handsome, popular guys on baseball and football teams couldn't accept that a weird nerd might take their chance to hold her hand in public, or something even better in private. He could have been comforted by a little anger at his friend for taking his own chance and hanging at her shoulder all night. But, the emptiness in Tommy's gut, his hopelessness, was a familiar feeling. He gave up before he even tried.

He tried to encourage himself to stay and looked in the cooler beside the table. Jumbled in the ice was Bud Light, Coors Light, and Natty Ice, which all tasted like piss. He would rather have nothing until he got home. He grabbed a chip and scooped up some salsa, but it was like biting into stale, wet cardboard. Most of the food must have been sitting there for a week. It was time to go. Without saying anything to anyone and without looking for his friend, he was about to slip out easily unnoticed.

The front door crashed open and black-masked men with guns yelled for everyone to "Get down!" as they fanned into the apartment and the back rooms. Girls screamed and hid their heads in their hands, guys hooted *what the fuck?* quietly to each other, and Tommy slid out the back door.

His friend was outside already. "Dude, we've got to get the fuck out of here!"

"Where's Amelia?"

"I don't know, but we gotta go."

"I'm not gonna leave her here."

"She'll be fine. Come on!" He crept into the shadows around the side of the house, but Tommy didn't follow, even when he saw his friend hop over the fence and run away.

Tommy peeked into every window until he found her hiding in an open closet in one of the bedrooms. The flat of his hands couldn't open the window, it must have been locked, so he knocked as quietly as he could. There was still screaming and yelling inside and she couldn't hear him. A stack of bricks along the fence waited for him, some of them happily ready to abandon the project that would never be finished and join him in this rescue. But he had to distract the gunmen first. Slowly, he opened the gate to the driveway and stepped around to the living room window, threw a brick into it, and ran back to Amelia. He threw a brick through that window and used another to scrape away all the broken glass. "Come on, come on," he whispered, but as she ran to him, one of the men came in from the hallway and grabbed her.

He pointed the gun at Tommy while pulling her away. "Get out of here, fatty!"

He froze, then when the man turned around, he threw himself like a clumsy brick into the shattered opening. Amelia fought to hold the gun away until Tommy grabbed it from behind and crushed the man's fingers like candy canes, then slammed his head into the wall. The body fell to the floor. Sirens could be heard getting closer and, hearing them, the other gunmen ran out of the house like cockroaches in a sudden flick of light. Amelia buried her face in Tommy's chest and they went through to where everyone was lifting their heads, trying to figure out what happened and if anyone was hurt. With one arm around her, he stopped at the table, grabbed another hamburger, and took a bite as they walked out of the house together. He would never deny being himself again.

My Mother Got Married

My brother is in alcohol. The bottle is too small. He is held by the taste and to numbness enthralled. I see him down the hall.

Last night, we celebrated our mother's wedding to a dangerous man. He never cares when we fall, but he makes a spectacle of our home's deep wall into which we are thrown and locked away until we can, repentant, crawl out through the hole and give him our all. I am ready, but my brother stashed a jug of something that makes him sadder and I don't know why. I asked if I could have a try and he let me, but it burned and I choked and coughed and our stepdad heard me and yelled at us to be quiet.

"I'm going," I tell my brother.

And he says, "don't."

I should've listened to him. He's been here longer. As soon as I creep out, my stepdad hits my head. My mother silently stays in her room. My brother silently stays in the dark. "I thought you said we can come out when we're ready to apologize." He hits my head again and I hear my brother shake his own head.

"I told you not to come out until I'm ready for you to apologize."

I slink back in and watch my brother's shadow. It barely moves because the drink would make a sound. I don't want to think about what he would do to us if what we had was found. I reach out my hand and he slowly gives me the bottle.

"Alright, get out!"

I stumble and drop it on the carpet. It splashes out of the small crawl hole and he hears and sees and smells it, but before I know any of that, he reaches in quickly and grabs my shirt to yank me out. It hurts my neck and he says not to pout. I'm in for much worse. My brother's still in there. I hope he rescues me. I hope he doesn't come out. Life's a curse and now I understand why he was drinking and always drinks and why he stopped thinking and smiling and dreaming. I wish my mom would come out and make him stop. I'm numb, but I only had one taste. I've tasted much worse at the end of a belt. I must be stronger, unless I'm dead.

He asks, "How many for stealing my whiskey, boy?"

And for some reason I say, "Eighteen."

"Ok, the age you can drink. Remember this next time you think you're a man."

I promise I'm not making it up. It didn't hurt at all. Then, I hear someone fall and turn around to see my mother. There's blood and a knife in her hand. I hope my brother is well enough to stand. He can. We walk out of the house and leave the dead man's dangerous body.

The Disappearance of Madeline

He knelt down when he noticed the bookmark, flimsy and half-bent, decorated with the bookstore's orange cat logo. The police had called off the search days ago, but they didn't know the secret places Madeline went. Ian knew. Those secret places were only for them. But, he broke their secret pact to find her. When he tried to tell the police to look in their hidden forest, they said they'd already looked there. But, he knew they hadn't. Why did they give up? He wouldn't stop looking, forever.

Among the tangled bushes, under the weaving trees, Ian stumbled in a daze. If he'd felt anything, it was like his life force had been drained when he wasn't looking. He felt nothing. He thought she might be dead. Sometimes, Madeline didn't wait at the stop sign after school, too excited to go to the forest, and Ian would run to meet her there. He always waited for her, though. This time, it was different. She wasn't there, but he didn't care to run, and when he crawled through the invisible entrance of hedges and vines, he was alone. Every day, he searched after school. Why did the police stop looking after they spoke to his mom? When Ian asked her, she answered, "You know why," without looking at him. She never looked at him. "Why won't you help me find her?" he asked and again she answered, "You know why."

He went past the magic wishing tree, but it seemed to be just a tree. It only looked like a tree. It didn't feel like a magic wishing tree, anymore. He crept behind the waterfall where the mist was somehow always warm. In the mossy cave where they used to sit and hold hands and watch the sunlight make rainbows on the water, it was cold. This was where they went to kiss. This was where they talked about staying together forever. But now, it was silent and empty. Where was she? His eyes began to fill with tears, but he held them in and went to the castle they were building. The jagged rocks standing in walls and piles ready to be added were all where they left them. He found Madeline's book in the little reading spot he'd made for her. He opened it and looked through the pages, remembering the last thing she read to him, and placed the bookmark there. One of the flat rocks they'd collected was perfect for a reading table and to hold a cup of tea. He'd meant to make it a surprise for her the next time they went to their castle. But instead of waiting, he carried the rock and put it in the soft grass in the perfect spot where she liked to sit.

The quarry where they collected rocks was nearby. He'd already searched there every day since she disappeared, but he went anyway to look again. From the forest ledge, he looked for a sign of her. It hadn't changed. Everything was where it had been since the last time they were here. But, this place felt different too. It felt like something was waiting for him. There was a blue color poking out from the jumbles of rock. He scrambled down the path of dirt and roots and though he couldn't see the color anymore, he moved the big stones one by one as quickly as he could, digging through them to find whatever it was. Finally, he found a blue jacket and yanked it out. The sleeve was scraped open and Ian could see blood on the torn hole. He rifled through the pockets and felt a piece of paper. He pulled it out and opened it to see a note written to him from Madeline, *I'll miss you.*

He took the jacket and note to the police station and felt relieved when they promised to examine it. For a few days he waited until they arrived at his house and he hid behind the couch where he could hear them speaking with his mother at the door.

"He brought these to us, but the blood on the jacket is his."

"This is the jacket he lost a few weeks ago."

"What about this?"

She sighed, dropping the paper note to her side.

"Ma'am, we understand this is a hard time for him, but it is strange that we've had no other reports of a missing girl."

"Because she doesn't exist! This is his handwriting."
She started to cry, gently, wishing for any sympathetic ear.
"It's like he's crazy. I don't know what to do with him."

"Would it be okay for us to talk to him?"

"I don't know what to do, anymore. I've tried to tell
him it's an imaginary friend, but he won't listen."

Ian was tired of hearing it. He'd heard it a million
times before. But she was real. He snuck quietly out the back
door and ran to the forest to continue looking. He didn't want
to admit that he felt like he'd never find her. When he got to
the castle, it was too dark to read, so he held her book on his
chest and fell asleep in the grass.

Looking through her son's torn jacket, his mother
found a library card with the title of the book he'd lost, the
one he said was Madeline's.

Little, Incremental Things

The cold coffee and bacon made Dennis feel like dried grease. The counter at the luncheonette was clean, but he was dirty. The fifties chrome and big windows reminded him of his son's favorite movie, set in a time of American paranoia but nonetheless remembered in its real-time nostalgia where boys lived forever riding bikes on their way to play baseball, jeans rolled up above bare feet gripping the spikey pedals and still wet from the creek. He saw the memory of those boys and swallowed his tears.

No one knew him here and so, regardless of how much hometown comfort this place seemed to have, it would be nothing to him. The waitress must have sensed his out-of-time mind. Only once she asked, "Would you like a bit more coffee, sugar?" and he barely shook his head, preferring the stale cup he deserved. She didn't speak to him again after that. His son would've loved this place. Dennis pictured him in the grave with his gashed head, still sad that his daddy could have done this to him. There were still tears in the corners of his little boy eyes, wishing they could hug and make it right. Down in the ground, he was still crying.

As far as anyone else knew, his son had disappeared in the woods. Maybe he had gotten lost or maybe taken by a bear or a wolf. The people in town had numerous theories while the search parties continued. But he knew. The stories of horrible, lifelong scars are always about fathers with a drinking problem. They're never about the little, incremental things that close in on a person's patience until it snaps.

His day at work had been relatively simple. Nothing unusual obstructed his flow and every joke in the break room seemed, though not actually very funny, humorous enough to laugh at. People had stopped talking to him quietly and carefully, they had stopped asking how he was doing, and the undertone of sympathy after his wife died backed away and let his friends treat him like a man again. His son wasn't as sure how to go about his life and was still alternating between brave ingenuity, like when he used the tree to create a pulley and hoist his bike up on the roof to then ride it off the edge, and despondent confusion where he moped around the house and didn't seem to hear a word his father said to him. The mess was piling up and Dennis was raising his voice more often, exhausted from a long day and then coming home to make a crunchy, oversalted dinner and try to teach his boy how to do the dishes. But the dishes were never clean and every time he turned around there were five more things on the floor to pick up; toys, dirty laundry, half an apple… They needed a vacation. When Dennis slapped his son across the face for the third time that week, he decided, that's enough. We need to get out of here and relax for a while.

"Make sure all your chores are done by the time I get home so we can hit the road." That morning, the boy's eyes looked up with half a bright smile, excited for their first father/son fishing trip, and Dennis felt like he was seeing him for the first time since his mother died. He'd been somewhere else, but now he was coming back.

After that relatively simple day at work, Dennis pulled into the driveway and saw his son's bike outside. Alright, it's not put away, but that's okay. Then, he walked in the front door and tripped on the toy he'd told his son to pick up earlier. He fell to the ground tangled in the appendage of his briefcase and jacket. Getting up, cussing, he noticed the pile of clothes, half on the table, half on the floor, which were supposed to be packed but instead were surrounded by muddy footprints. He went through the screen door to the backyard where the hose was uncoiled in the grass and its brass sprinkler head was trickling water.

His son ran around the corner of the house, "Hi, dad!"

"What the fuck is all this mess?! I told you to have everything clean before I got back." He felt a heat overwhelm his brain as he bent down to pick up the hose.

"I was…"

"I FUCKIN told you!" and he cracked his son's head with the brass end of the hose.

Dennis hasn't cried since then, not while he packed his son into the car that night, not while he buried him deep in the ground far away from town. He felt like nothing more than a body. His son was more alive than him. He despised himself and he wished there was a way to undo what he'd done. After aiding the search parties in the forest where they were supposed to go fishing, after waiting enough time and then telling enough people he might need to move away because the pain was too heavy, after planting those seeds that everyone could accept, he left town.

"Sugar, would you like a box for your food? We need to close soon."

Dennis didn't say a word. He slipped off the bench and walked out the door. A few boys rode around him on their bikes and he could feel the misery welling up behind his eyes and in his throat, but he held it down. He was certain that if he let one tear escape, he would cry until he died. He wished he could safely kill himself, but he dreaded knowing that he would be immediately face to face with his son.

The Weight of Gold

One day while travelling through the woods, the tribe came to a disturbing sight, a wall cutting through the forest higher than the trees and as far as they could see. Fìrinn turned to the nearest tree and asked, "Tree, what is this and what is beyond?"

"I hear much noise beyond," the tree replied, "and sense none of my kind since their pain long ago."

The tribe resolved to seek into this disrupting creation. The men, women, and children took turns kicking and slamming into the wall, cracking it, breaking it, until at last they opened a hole large enough for them to pass through one by one.

The women shrieked, the children were frightened, the men were tearful and confused. They saw a flat, grey void stretching into a far, hazy horizon. The ground their feet stood on was harder and rougher than stone. The air stung their eyes and smelled so horrible they could barely breathe.

A man appeared and shouted at them, "What do you think you're doing?!" He was grossly slouched. Piled upon his back were strapped big, roughly hewn rocks of gold.

One girl from the tribe was immediately enamored by the bright stones. Fìrinn tried to call her back, but her mother was captivated too and joined her in admiring them. Noticing the look in their eyes, the deformed man promised them a chip of gold in return for repairing the wall they had broken. He made the same offer to the whole tribe, but Fìrinn led them on, sadly leaving the two who remained.

They kept close to the wall, looking out at the concrete nothingness and hearing a distant roaring sound which had not ceased. No breeze nor rustling of leaves, no birdsong, the sky and the ground were the same dull shade. They passed more of these strange people with gold boulders upon their backs and gold rocks hanging around their necks, these strange people who shouted at the tribe and called them names they did not understand. But some were kinder and offered to show them their rocks and how they achieved them. Eventually, all the tribe was enticed to walk into the wasteland, and Fìrinn was alone.

He continued along the wall himself. It seemed an endless continuance of night-day. When he hungered, he broke through the wall into the forest where he could fill his belly and rest. Yet still, he wanted to explore this strange land. He'd watched his people succumb and disappear in many directions. His journey wasn't done.

For a long while, he travelled without seeing a single person. Then he saw a sort-of woman, bent from her load of gold strapped to her shoulders and her two children running circles around her. When they wandered a few steps away, she barked at them and they returned to her ankles. He saw them begin to wrestle at her feet, then she barked again and held a tiny piece of gold in front of their face while talking in a low voice until they sat silent and still. The woman caught sight of Fìrinn and gave a terrible shriek, "Put some clothes on, you pervert!"

She pulled the children away into the expanse as they tried to look back. Fìrinn walked on, confused. When he saw a man sitting on the ground nearby twiddling his fingers and talking to himself, he approached cautiously. Softly, he asked the man if he was alright, the man who was not startled at seeing Fìrinn because he never looked at him, but kept staring at the ground as they talked.

"Why was that woman frightened of my body?"

"Your body? What body?" said the man, who still did not look up.

Fìrinn replied sarcastically, "What might someone see when they take a look around?"

"Haha, yes," said the man, "Some are so blind."

Fìrinn was slightly entertained by this ridiculously unaware man. He saw golden rocks hanging not just around his neck, but also from his wrists and sleeves and worn as rings, and he noticed the man could not rise from under the weight of his giant robe. "What would you say to a man only dressed in his skin?"

The man chuckled, "Such a man who would go around nude must be mad or wishing for death. What would protect him from the elements?" He still did not look up from the ground.

"When the day is beautiful?"

"Does it matter? It's disgusting. Besides, it's illegal."

Fìrinn did not understand the word. "What makes it so?"

"It's indecent."

Illegal because it's indecent. Indecent because it's illegal. The words seemed to mean nothing and Fìrinn decided to continue on. He bid the man farewell, who did not answer, but continued talking to himself and twiddling his thumbs.

Fìrinn was urinating against the wall, then turned around to see a man standing behind him. This one did not have any gold and stood with shoulders slouching like one very depressed. His face was sour like all those Fìrinn had met in this place. "Do you want to be arrested?" He motioned with a hand and led Fìrinn in a hurried walk. They went to where cornered grey walls enclosed a space with more walls and doors inside. "I'll keep watch while you use the toilet."

"Toilet?"

The man led him inside and showed him the bowls and how the lever flushed. Fìrinn was disgusted at the waste of fresh water. "Why?" he asked.

"Should the ground be covered in it? How gross."

"Only because the ground is covered with this." Fìrinn said, stomping the concrete with his foot.

The man looked puzzled. "Hurry, before someone catches us. We clearly don't have the stuff to pay for this."

Fìrinn had finished on the wall, so he looked at the bowls for a moment before coming out from the stalls. "You don't carry the rocks I've seen."

"I had gold, more than most. But, I was foolish and gambled until I lost it all. Now, I'm a poor man."

They walked together for a while and the man tried to show Fìrinn where those without gold gather, but he refused to leave the wall, which the man seemed too eager to get away from. They came upon a large crowd and the man scuttled away frightened, waving "good luck" to the stranger.

Men and women were huddled close with hordes of gold upon their backs and all talking without looking at each other. In the center of the throng was a towering pillar of gold. "What is this?" Fìrinn asked himself out loud.

Someone heard and suddenly the mob couldn't stifle their uproar of laughter. They continued laughing and moving away. "What is this?" he asked of someone still looking in his direction as he approached.

A gold-laden man appeared very embarrassed and looked around as if for help, but everyone was shying away. "This is the late John Smith." he said, trying to hide his laughter.

"Oh, I see," said Fìrinn sympathetically, "I did not mean to interrupt your grieving."

"Haha! No grief of mine. We're constructing his tomb."

"Are these his loved ones?"

"We're working. Building rich men's graves pays well."

"He must have been very lonely to have only slaves here and none who mourn him."

"Ha! What are you talking about? Look at his wealth!"

"What are you looking at?" Fìrinn shouted, suddenly overcome, "A rotting corpse and a pile of rocks!" He had the attention of some, who were slightly entertained. He walked to an uncarved heap of gold, nearly as tall as the tower. Beneath laid a dead man. "I suppose no one knows this man, either?"

"Nope, he's been there a while."

"Look how young his face is."

"But, look how much he achieved."

Fìrinn gave the man an angry look and he backed away, frightened. "Does anyone here know these dead men?!" he yelled, raising himself up, "Does anyone know the person next to you?! You're huddled so close, yet…" he heard sarcastic snickering and threw up his hands.

Weary, walking alone, he was ready to return to the forest. Then, he heard an old man's terrible coughing. He approached and kneeled beside the white-haired elder, who was cringing and shivering. "Any change you can spare, young man?"

Fìrinn replied softly, "Change spares no one."

The old man said no more.

"Perhaps, I can take you to your family."

"I don't know where they are."

"Is there some way I can help you?"

"There's a lake I've dreamed of seeing since I was a boy…" The old man coughed and it hurt so much he gave up saying more.

Fìrinn lifted the man up and he whimpered from the pain. The weight of him was like a dry leaf. Soon, they arrived at the beautiful, glistening water. The wall rounded the sandy shore and a few sat on the beach leaning against their giant loads of gold.

Fìrinn carried the old man across the sand and they were suddenly accosted by a round and raging man, "Get the hell off my property! Filthy bums!" Fìrinn gave the man's knee a sharp kick and he fell fast to the ground, his shout of pain cut short as he was crushed by his golden boulders.

Sitting the elderly man near the water, Fìrinn noticed a rowboat and dragged it over. He placed him quietly in it and they rowed out to the middle of the lake where they sat and relaxed. The old man put his hands in the water, smiling. "Thank you," he said, "I want to give you something for your help." The old man pulled out two small, golden rocks from his pocket and gave them to Fìrinn. He accepted the gift graciously, then tossed them into the water. Painfully, the old man jerked in dismay and watched them sink. Then, he smiled, breathed a deep slow sigh, and laid with his face looking up to the sunlight.

Fìrinn looked at him happily for a long moment. His eyes did not reopen. Taking the oar, he bashed a hole in the bottom of the boat. Water rushed in. The boat and the old man's body sank as Fìrinn swam to shore. He broke through the wall and climbed back into the forest, where he remained.

A young girl snuck away from her vigilant parents and was exploring around the lake. She saw the hole in the wall and cautiously peered in. Wild trees, birds singing their afternoon song, the smell of soil and leaves and flowers. She looked to make sure no one was watching and then crawled through.

The Poem

Atop a summit
immortals dwelt
in a hidden temple
through rumored mountains
of sheer cliffsides
and icy winds howling.
The strictest order
of enlightenment
transforming laymen to gods.
First in the code, every monk
was free to leave at will,
but only in exile.
Another rule within the walls,
no mortal was permitted
the reciting or inscribing of verse.
One monk refused this rule
and during his times of solitude
he hid invisible in the farthest alcove
of the labyrinthine gardens,
slowly and silently etching a poem
in a stone which stood
amidst untended overgrowth.
One day, night fell.
And in that night
after thousands of years in stoic secrecy
the temple burned, every timber, to ash.
Some ran from the temple gate.
Some, from the first sight of flames,
leapt from the ledges into the clouds.
Only the stone, alone, remains
with a simple poem -

and yet